THE BIG
SNEEZE

For my father, Hugh Antonsen

Copyright ©1985 by Ruth Brown.
This paperback edition first published in 2002 by Andersen Press Ltd.
The rights of Ruth Brown to be identified as the author and illustrator of this work
have been asserted by her in accordance with the Copyright, Designs and Patents Act, 1988.
First published in Great Britain in 1985 by Andersen Press Ltd. 20 Vauxhall Bridge Road, London SW1V 2SA.
Published in Australia by Random House Australia Pty., 20 Alfred Street, Milsons Point, Sydney, NSW 2061.
All rights reserved. Colour separated in Switzerland by Photolitho AG, Zurich.
Printed and bound in Italy by Grafiche AZ, Verona.

10 9 8 7 6 5 4 3 2 1

British Library Cataloguing in Publication Data available.

ISBN 1 84270 090 1

This book has been printed on acid-free paper

THE BIG SNEEZE
Ruth Brown

Andersen Press • London

One hot afternoon, the farmer and his animals were dozing in the barn. The only sound was the buzz-buzz of a lazy fly.

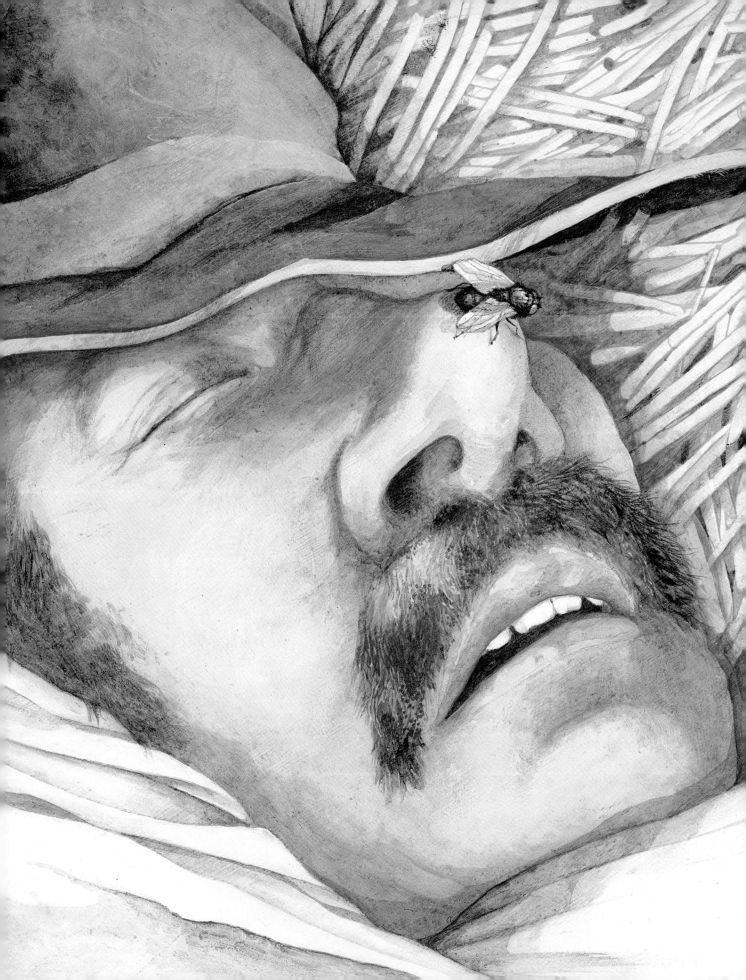

Suddenly the buzzing stopped –
the fly had landed right on the end of the farmer's nose!

"ATISHOOOOOOOOOOO!" the farmer sneezed so hard
that the fly was blown high up into a spider's web.

This disturbed the spider,
who captured the fly –

which alerted the sparrow,
who chased the spider.

This wakened the cat,
who leapt at the bird –

which woke the dog,
and frightened the rats –

who fled from the barn,
chased by the dog –

which scattered the startled
hens from their roost –

and panicked the terrified donkey!

"What on earth have you done?" shrieked the farmer's wife.

"Nothing, my dear," replied the farmer. "I only sneezed!"

More Andersen Press paperback picture books!

Scarecrow's Hat
by Ken Brown

Funny Fred
by Peta Coplans

Dear Daddy
by Philippe Dupasquier

War and Peas
by Michael Foreman

The Monster and the Teddy Bear
by David McKee

Princess Camomile Gets Her Way
by Hiawyn Oram and Susan Varley

Bear's Eggs
by Dieter and Ingrid Schubert

Rabbit's Wish
by Paul Stewart and Chris Riddell

The Sand Horse
by Ann Turnbull and Michael Foreman

Frog and a Very Special Day
by Max Velthuijs

Dr Xargle's Book of Earth Hounds
by Jeanne Willis and Tony Ross